Dinosaur Brains is dedicated to the Lord Jesus Christ who is the giver of all gifts and the inspiration of all I do. It is also dedicated to my family who encourages and supports me in all my endeavors and gently points out when I'm allowing my dinosaur brain to get in my way. To my ride or die peeps; Lovey, Siti, Mark, Mogo, Beans, Mandib, Milga, Carmencita, San, Rizzard, and Lin. I love you all.

Thank you especially to Alex Howell for his code writing skills.

-Tabitha

www.mascotbooks.com

Dinosaur Brains

For more information, please contact:
Mascot Books
560 Herndon Parkway #120
Herndon, VA 20170
info@mascotbooks.com

Library of Congress Control Number: 2015904998

CPSIA Code: PRT0515A
ISBN-13: 978-1-62086-950-5

Printed in the United States

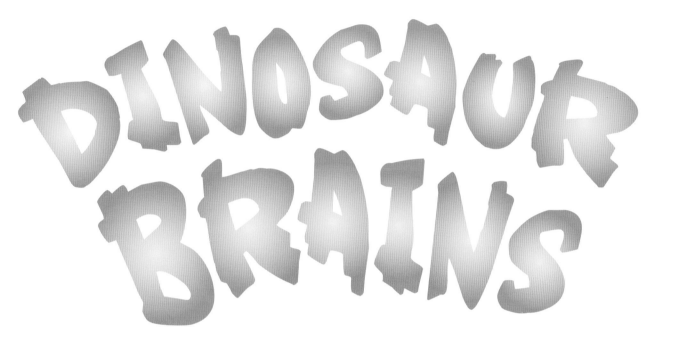

Tabitha Renée Mann
illustrated by Susan Robinson

Grandpa was worried when he heard someone crying in the living room. He put down his paper and ran to the door to see Tabbie, his granddaughter, crying. "What's the matter, sweetheart?" he asked.

"I can't do my homework because there are no chubby, black swimmers in the Olympics!" she wailed.

"Huh?" said Grandpa, confused.

"I have to write about what I want to be when I grow up. But Robbie said there are no chubby, black Olympic swimmers, but I love to swim! Robbie's right, going to the Olympics is a silly dream!" Tabbie cried.

"Umph! Sounds like dinosaur brains have gotten a hold of you. That's a pity," Grandpa said and walked out of the room.

"Dinosaur brain?! What do you mean?" asked Tabbie, wiping her tears and following Grandpa.

"Well," Grandpa started, sitting in his comfy, old chair, "there are two types of brains. Your human brain that dreams great dreams like becoming an Olympic swimmer, and your dinosaur brain. That's the brain talking now."

"Two brains? Dinosaur brain? Nu-uhhh!" Tabbie sniffled and crawled into his lap.

"It's true!" said Grandpa, hugging the little girl as they settled in for a story.

"A long, long, loooong time ago, there was a man named Glub…"

Glub gathered all of his friends and family to tell them about the wonderful things he'd dreamed of. Picking up his son Little G, he said, "Son! You know how you always want to sleep with me and your mom?"

"Yeah, Dad. But only because it's cold at night!" Little G said defensively as he heard his friends snicker and call him Baby G.

"Well," Glub said, "this new thing will make it really warm at night, and it brings light to the darkness, just in case someone is afraid of the dark. I'm thinking of calling it...fire."

As ooooohs and aaaaaaahs began stirring the group, Glub continued, "But that's not all! Pug!" Glub said startling his best friend, "You know how our arms are always sore from carrying the food we catch?"

"Do I ever!" the scrawny little caveman said rubbing his sore muscles.

"Well, with this new thing - the wheel - we'll be able to umm...roll stuff instead of carry it! Like this, see?"

Glub launched himself down a hill demonstrating how the wheel would work. The entire village cheered at the idea of never lifting heavy loads again. One by one they all rolled down the hill following Glub.

At the bottom of the hill they all talked excitedly about fire and the wheel until Little G noticed that Glub had suddenly gone quiet.

"What's wrong, Dad?"

"Well," Glub said, "I have another idea and it's the most exciting one! It sounds really crazy, but it's this thing called writing."

Just as Glub began to describe how writing would allow them to record forever all the great Uncle Rugbus stories that everyone loved so much, a giant dinosaur came and…

CRUNCH! gobbled him up.

His friends screamed and ran for cover. They were convinced
the dinosaur ate him because of his outrageous dreams, especially
the dream about writing! After that, no one wanted anything to do
with Glub's dangerous ideas, except Aooga.

"Those thoughts will bring nothing but trouble!" people warned.
But still, Aooga took Glub's ideas and made them his own.

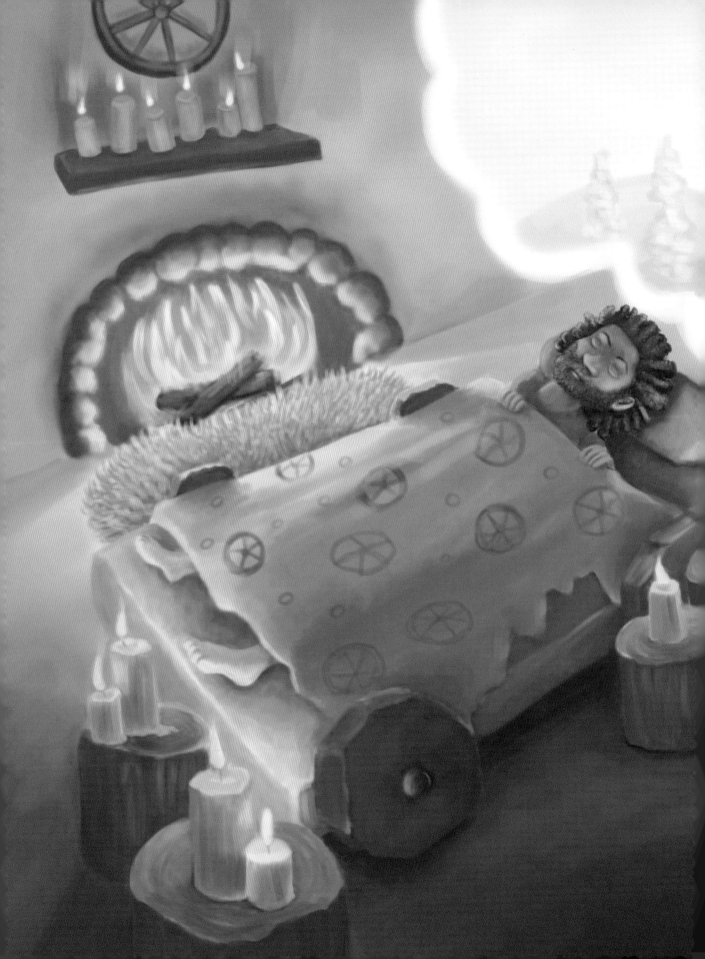

"What happened to Aooga?" Tabbie asked.

"He followed his dreams. He eventually did discover fire and the wheel, changing the world forever. Sadly though, Aooga's dinosaur brain told him that writing was crazy and impossible, so he never discovered writing."

"But…?" said Tabbie, holding up a book full of words written on a page.
"But Aooga's great granddaughter, Chichachooga, overcame the fear
and finally discovered writing."

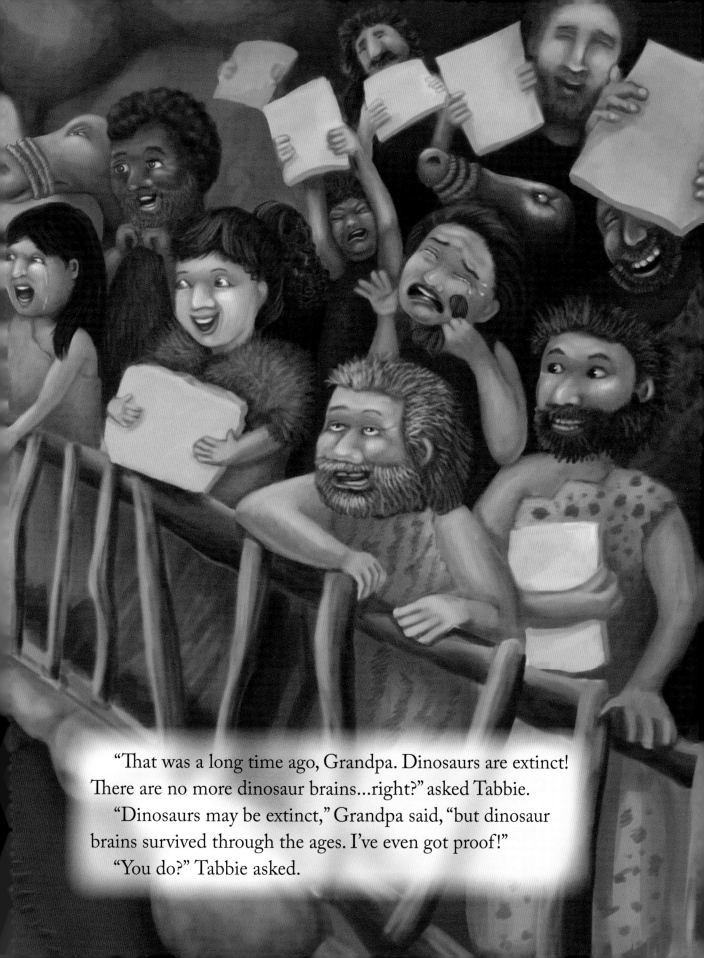

"That was a long time ago, Grandpa. Dinosaurs are extinct! There are no more dinosaur brains...right?" asked Tabbie.

"Dinosaurs may be extinct," Grandpa said, "but dinosaur brains survived through the ages. I've even got proof!"

"You do?" Tabbie asked.

"Have you ever heard of Sir Bama Lama?"

"We haven't studied him in school yet, I don't think."

"He was the first person to think of the telephone. How about Marybeth Johnson? She was the first person to think of hiding runaway slaves in a series of houses until they reached freedom in the North. What about Bling Shtell, the first person to think of over 300 uses for the peanut?"

"Nu-uhhh, Grandpa! Alexander Graham Bell did the telephone. Harriet Tubman freed slaves with the Underground Railroad and George Washington Carver was the peanut man! We just studied that and I got an A on the test, so I know!" Tabbie said proudly.

"They were the first to do it, not the first to think it. Dinosaur brains got to Bama Lama, Miss Johnson, and Bling Shtell…gobbled their dreams right up."

"Ooooohhhhh!" said Tabbie, understanding now. "And we still have dinosaur brains today?"

"You betcha! Put on these glasses and you can see them," said Grandpa, handing her a pair. Tabbie ran to the window and looked outside.

There, Tabbie was amazed to see a T-rex chasing a mailman who dreamed of playing the guitar in front of a crowd of people. A long-neck was eating Mrs. Lovell's dream of owning a home with a big backyard and a wrap-around porch. A raptor swooped down on her friend Camille's dream of becoming the President of the United States. Everywhere she looked, Tabbie saw dinosaurs gobbling up dreams.

"Wow, Grandpa, I never knew about dinosaur brains! Hey, what happened to Glub's family and friends?" she asked.

"Oh, they're still around. Instead of letting their dinosaur brains eat only their dreams, they've become like dinosaurs themselves, discouraging others and eating their dreams, too."

"Like Robbie!"

"Yep, just like Robbie. The only way to beat them is to walk away from them."

"Won't they bite?"

"They'll try, but there's one surefire thing that will make them go away…"

"What? What? What?"

YOU SHOULD JUST GIVE IT UP.

YEAH, MAYBE GLUB COULD'VE MADE THE WHEEL.

GLUB WAS SMARTER THAN YOU.

"Imagine the dinosaurs all tied up and powerless. Then say to yourself, 'I have power, love, and self-control – NO FEAR!' and they will leave you alone."

"Thanks, Grandpa! I think I'll go write my paper now!"

"Go get 'em, tiger!" Grandpa said as he settled in for a nice nap.

Don't be afraid. You have been given
power, love, and self-control.

ABOUT THE AUTHOR

Tabitha Mann is a clinical social worker in Northern Virginia. She helps people conquer the fears that keep them from achieving their goals. In 2010 she was listed among DC's Top Ten Story Tellers by SpeakeasyDC. She has dreamed of being a writer since she was a child, but her dinosaur brain always told her that writing professionally was something other people did – not what she could do – until now.

With *Dinosaur Brains* she has conquered her fear and followed her dream. Tabitha hopes this book will encourage you to follow your dreams without (or even in spite of) your fears because God has not given us a spirit of fear but of power, love, and self-control. *(2 Peter 1:7)*